Published by Top That! Publishing plc
Tide Mill Way, Woodbridge, Suffolk, IP12 1AP, UK
www.topthatpublishing.com
Illustration copyright © Sam McPhillips 2011
Text copyright © Clemency Pearce 2011
All rights reserved
0 2 4 6 8 9 7 5 3 1
Printed and bound in China

Creative Director—Simon Couchman
Editorial Director—Daniel Graham

Illustrated by Sam McPhillips
Written by Clemency Pearce

ISBN 978-1-84956-881-4

Printed and bound in China

The Silent Owl

Illustrated by Sam McPhillips   Written by Clemency Pearce

For Rob and Silkie—Sam
For Gemma, the noisiest bird I know—CP

In the great, old hollow oak,
Lived an owl, who never spoke.

Fox asked, "Why do you never speak?"
But Owl refused to move his beak.

Squirrel scolded, "Are you nuts?"
But Owl ignored his toothy tuts.

Rat cried, "Owl! This isn't right!"
But Owl just gazed into the night.

Stag said, "Owl! We need a sign,
To let us know that you are fine."

So all the creatures gathered around,
To see if Owl would make a sound.

They stared at Owl; he stared right back.
Who would be the first to crack?

Stag declared, "He must be mute,
Or he doesn't give a hoot!"

At this, the owl produced a trumpet,
A big bass drum and stick to thump it.

Although Owl wouldn't hoot,
he played the bongos,

piano,

guitar,

and flute!

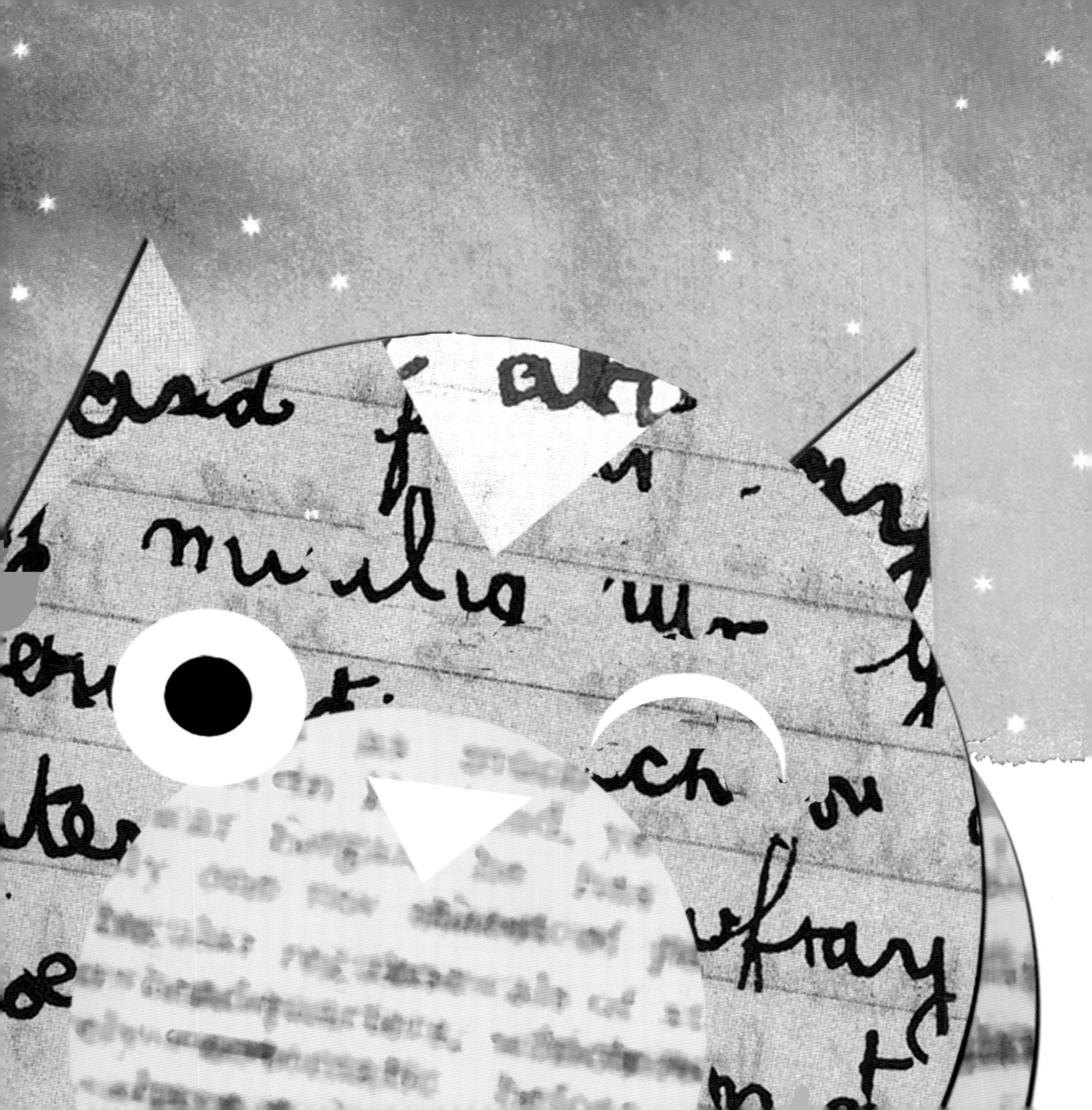